B48 755 326 9

KT-144-970

Milly and Molly

For my grandchildren
Thomas, Harry, Ella and Madeleine

Milly, Molly and The Tree Hut

Published by
Milly Molly Books
P O Box 539
Gisborne, New Zealand
email: books@millymolly.com

Printed by Rhythm Consolidated Berhad, Malaysia

ISBN: 1-86972-013-X

10 9 8 7 6 5 4 3 2 1

Milly, Molly and the Tree Hut

"We may look different
but we feel the same."

Milly and Molly's friend Maxter was a TV junkie. Maxter watched TV in the living room.

He watched TV in bed.

He watched TV before school,

after school,

on wet days

and, worst of all, on sunny days.

Until one sunny day his mother snapped.
"Maxter," she bellowed, "go outside
and exercise."

“Exercise how?” sulked Maxter.
“Exercise anyhow you like. The TV’s going off and I don’t want to see you until it is almost dark.”

With that, Maxter's mother shooed
Milly and Molly and Maxter out the door
and shut it.

“I know what we’ll do,” Milly said thoughtfully.

“What?” grumped Maxter.

“We’ll build a tree hut.”

“How?”scoffed Maxter.

“I know how,” said Molly.

“Yeah, right,” said Maxter. “Show me.”

Milly found the right tree. Molly helped Maxter find all the things they needed. Boards and boxes, a hammer and nails, and an old piece of canvas.

Milly, Molly and Maxter clambered, lifted
and hammered until it was almost dark.
“Well, well, well,” said Maxter’s mother.
“What a magnificent tree hut.”

Maxter went straight to bed. He was too tired for TV.

He was out of bed and back in his tree hut
before school. He couldn't be bothered with TV.

He went into his tree hut after school,

on wet days

and sunny days. He had no time for TV.

Then one day, after school, he heard a commotion. From his tree hut he could see boys playing football in the park.

“I want to play football,” he said.
“Well, well, well,” said Maxter’s mother
and she helped him sign up for a team.

If Maxter wasn't in his tree hut, he was playing football. He'd forgotten TV.

From the tree hut, Milly and Molly watched Maxter play football in the park. When he won Man Of The Match, they were sure they could hear Maxter's mother say "well, well, well".

“I’m going to be a football star when I grow up,” said Maxter.
“Will you be on TV?” asked Milly and Molly.
“I sure will,” said Maxter. “I won’t be watching TV, I’ll be on TV.”

"Well, well, well," said Maxter's mother.
"It's amazing what exercise can do."

PARENT GUIDE

Milly, Molly and the Tree Hut

The value implicitly expressed in this story is 'exercise'- physical exertion.

Milly and Molly help turn Maxter's life around. Maxter enjoys the benefit of exercise and the purpose it gives his life.

"We may look different but we feel the same".

Other picture books in the Milly, Molly series include:

- Milly, Molly and Jimmy's Seeds — ISBN 1-86972-007-5
- Milly, Molly and Pet Day — ISBN 1-86972-010-5
- Milly, Molly and Oink — ISBN 1-86972-009-1
- Milly and Molly Taffy Bogle — ISBN 1-86972-008-3
- Milly, Molly and Betelgeuse — ISBN 1-86972-011-3